Nuptse & Lhotse
Go to the
Rockies

Jocey Asnong

RMB

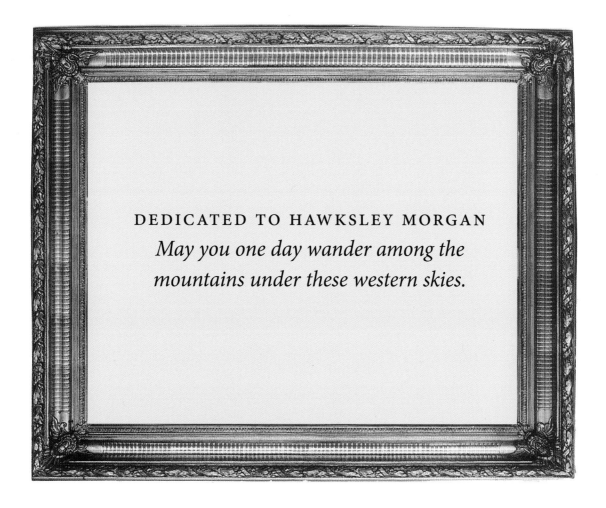

DEDICATED TO HAWKSLEY MORGAN
May you one day wander among the mountains under these western skies.

Once upon a time, not so very long ago, there lived two adventurous cats, Nuptse and Lhotse.

THINGS ABOUT NUPTSE (*Nup-see*):

Named after Mount Nuptse, a mountain right beside Mount Everest,

afraid of strawberry jam,

a scaredy cat,

a dreamer,

LOVES JELLYBEANS.

THINGS ABOUT LHOTSE (*Low-zee*):

Named after Mount Lhotse, a mountain right behind Mount Everest,

great at sports,

collects stamps,

a smarty pants,

LOVES BOOKS.

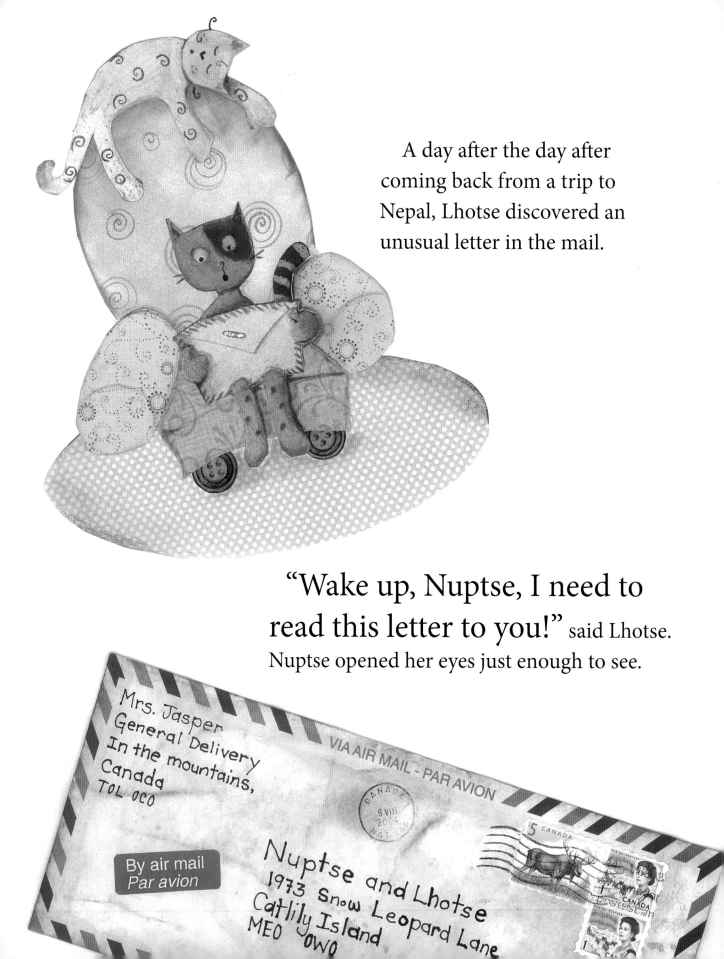

A day after the day after coming back from a trip to Nepal, Lhotse discovered an unusual letter in the mail.

"Wake up, Nuptse, I need to read this letter to you!" said Lhotse. Nuptse opened her eyes just enough to see.

Mrs. Jasper
General Delivery
In the mountains,
Canada
TOL 0C0

VIA AIR MAIL - PAR AVION

By air mail
Par avion

Nuptse and Lhotse
1973 Snow Leopard Lane
Catlily Island
MEO 0W0

$5 CANADA

dear Nuptse and Lhotse,

My name is Mrs. Jasper and I am a Grizzly Bear. I live in the Canadian Rockies. I heard that you are very good at climbing mountains and I need your help.

My little twin cubs, Yoho and Kootenay, (Yo-ho) (Koo-ten-aye) are lost! We had just left our hibernation cave in Paradise Valley and on our way to the Valley of the Ten Peaks, they went missing. Can you please come to the Rockies and help me find my children?

yours truly

Mrs. Jasper

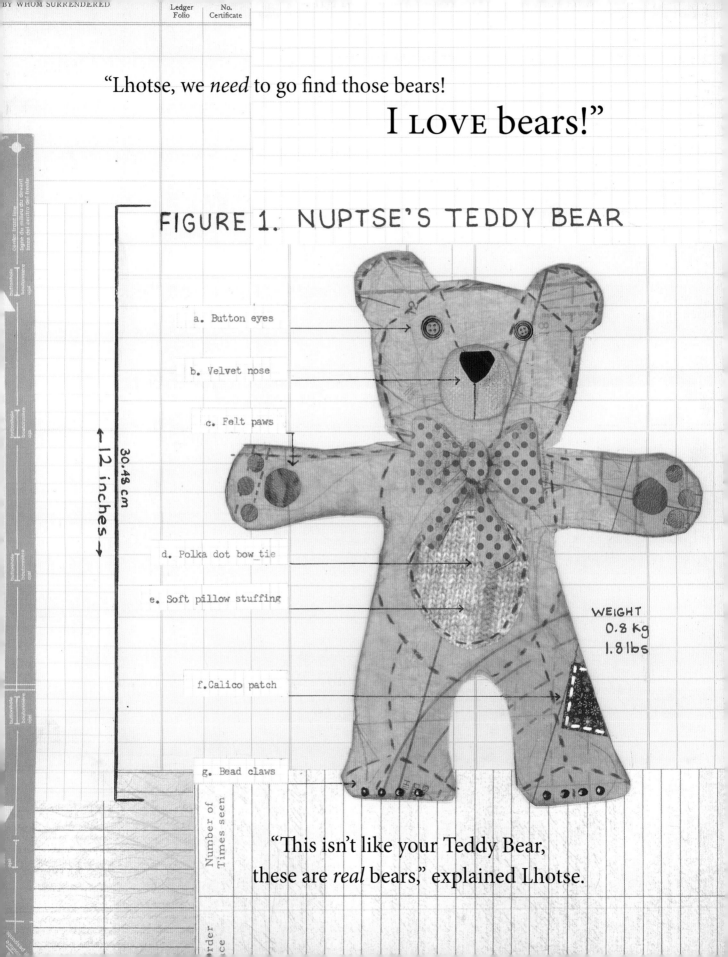

"Lhotse, we *need* to go find those bears! I LOVE bears!"

FIGURE 1. NUPTSE'S TEDDY BEAR

a. Button eyes

b. Velvet nose

c. Felt paws

d. Polka dot bow tie

e. Soft pillow stuffing

f. Calico patch

g. Bead claws

12 inches

30.48 cm

WEIGHT
0.8 kg
1.8 lbs

"This isn't like your Teddy Bear, these are *real* bears," explained Lhotse.

"Bears are **very big** and **very hungry** and **very fast** and I heard they don't like cats very much," said Lhotse.

FIGURE 2: A VERY REAL GRIZZLY BEAR

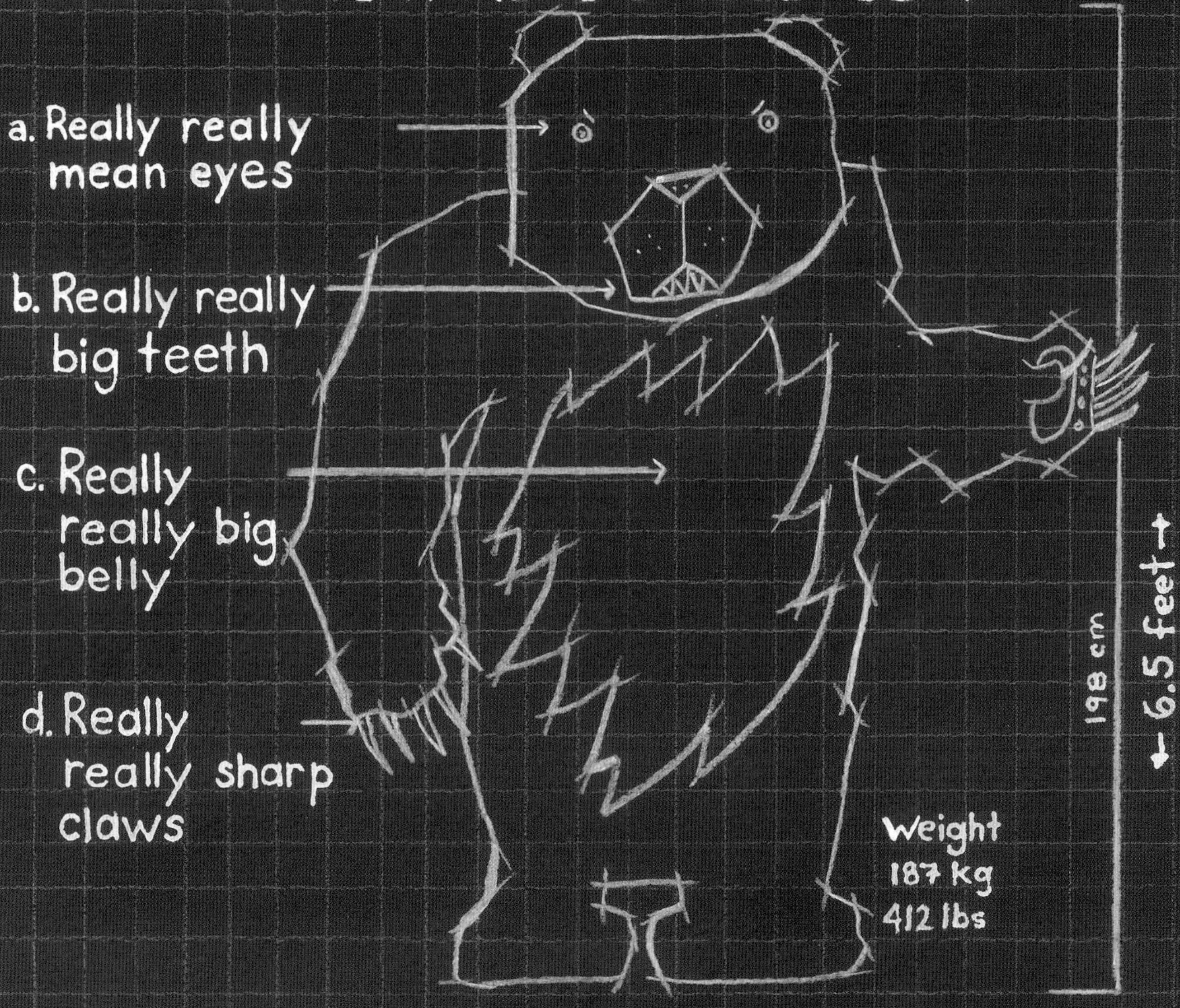

a. Really really mean eyes

b. Really really big teeth

c. Really really big belly

d. Really really sharp claws

198 cm

← 6.5 feet →

Weight
187 kg
412 lbs

"But she asked us to come. We have to help her. **Let's go!**" said Nuptse.

The cats travelled
through cities
and towns
and farms
and prairies
and forests
and around lakes
and over hills

and **FINALLY**
they arrived in the Rockies.

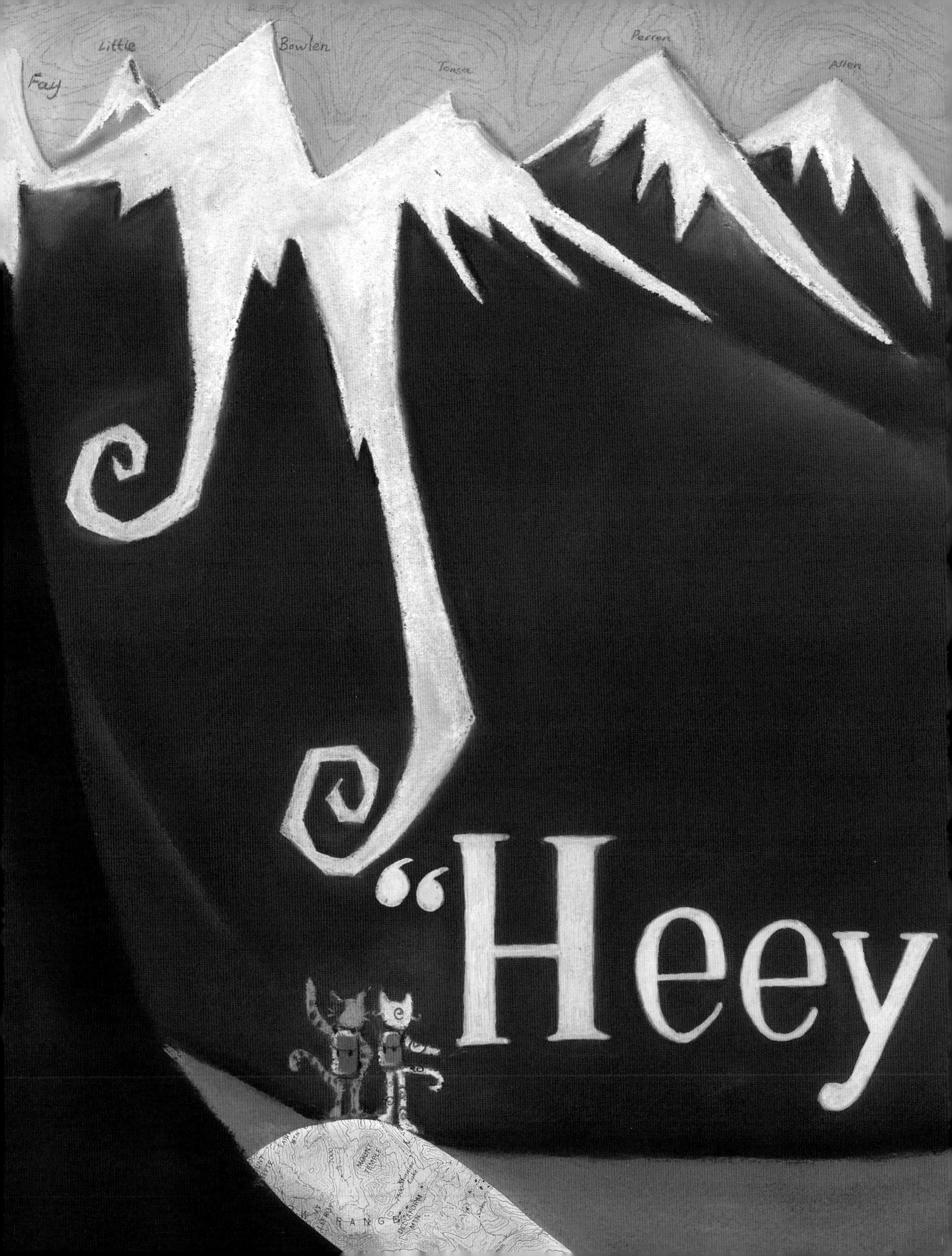
Fay
Little
Bowlen
Tonsa
Perren
Allen
“Heey
RANGE

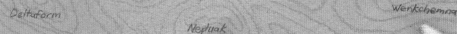

Tuzo Deltaform Neptuak Wenkchemna

Nuptse and Lhotse looked at the wall of
mountains known as the Valley of the Ten Peaks.
 "How do you think we'll find this grizzly bear?"
asked Lhotse.

Bearrrrr"

"HEY

The most gigantic bear the cats could have ever imagined was sitting right behind them. She was crying so hard that she had made puddles of tears around her.

It was Mrs. Jasper.

Caaats"

"This is the last place I saw Kootenay and Yoho," cried Mrs. Jasper.
"We were all eating berries together."

"I have an idea, let's look for clues," suggested Lhotse. The cats looked around the bushes carefully.

"I found some footprints!"

said Nuptse excitedly.
"They go down toward that lake!"

They followed the footprints to a group of canoes at the edge of the lake.

"Why does this water look so turquoise blue?" Lhotse asked.

"The water comes from glaciers as they melt in the summer," said Mrs. Jasper. "It's extremely cold and filled with rock flour."

"Rock FLOWER! Like daisies and lilies and roses?"
laughed Nuptse.

"No, not that kind of flower! It's called rock flour
because it looks like the flour that you use to bake a cake,"
explained Mrs. Jasper.

"I love cakes! Does this water taste like a cake?"
asked Nuptse.

Suddenly, Nuptse stood up in the canoe. "I think I see the cubs!" She pointed excitedly at the shore.

"Nuptse, sit down or you're going to tip the canoe," shouted Lhotse.

It was too late!

The canoe rocked then flipped over!

Splash

Mrs. Jasper swam as fast as a fish toward the cats. "Climb onto my back and I'll swim us all to shore," she said.

"I-I-I-I am turning into an i-i-i-icicle,"
shivered Nuptse.
"W-w-we need to get w-w-warm
before we catch a c-c-cold," said Lhotse
between chattering teeth.
"I know just where we should go to
warm up," said Mrs. Jasper. She climbed
up a hill and through a meadow of
flowers to a cozy cave.

The cats had just curled up
against the bear to dream deeply
when the loudest sound they had
ever heard shook the den.
"I think Mrs. Jasper is snoring!"
said Lhotse.

"I'm NOT snoring," growled Mrs. Jasper. "It's a train. The tracks are just below us. Yoho and Kootenay love watching trains. They always wanted to ride one to see where it went."

Lhotse suddenly had the funny look he got when he solved a hard math problem.

"I think I know where your bears went!" he exclaimed. **"We need to find a train station right away!"**

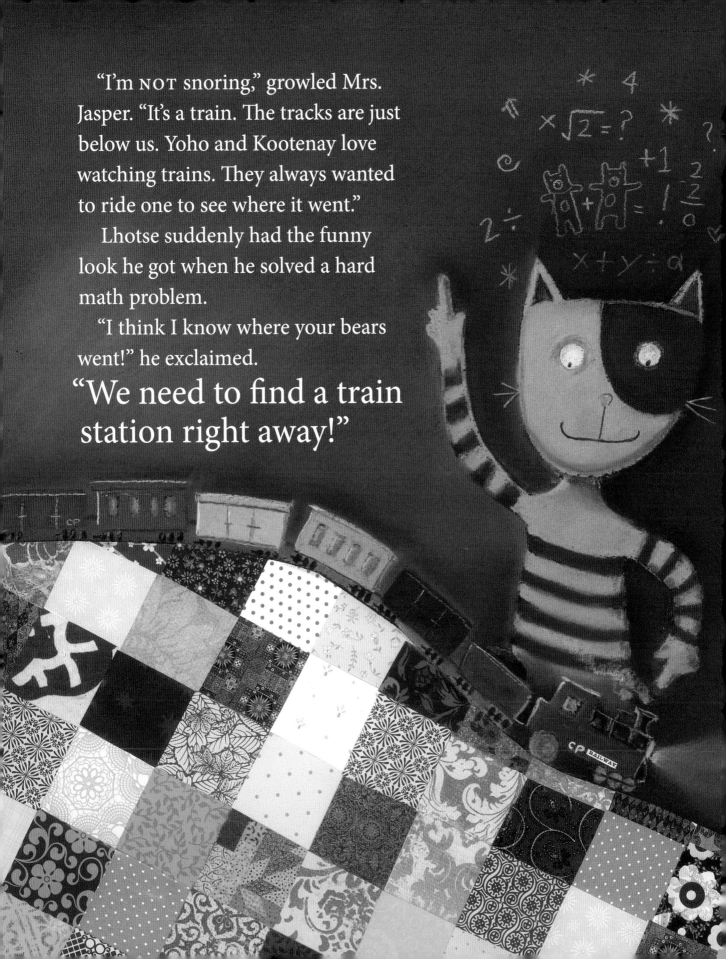

Under the glow of the northern lights, they snuck onto a train that was getting ready to leave the Banff station. With a loud whistle, the train began to rattle and roll and climb up through the Rocky Mountains.

The train did not slow down until the sun began to rise.

"I see the cubs!" said Nuptse when they were at the top of a snow-covered mountain.

"I see them, too!" said Mrs. Jasper.

"So do I!" said Lhotse.

"Let's jump!"

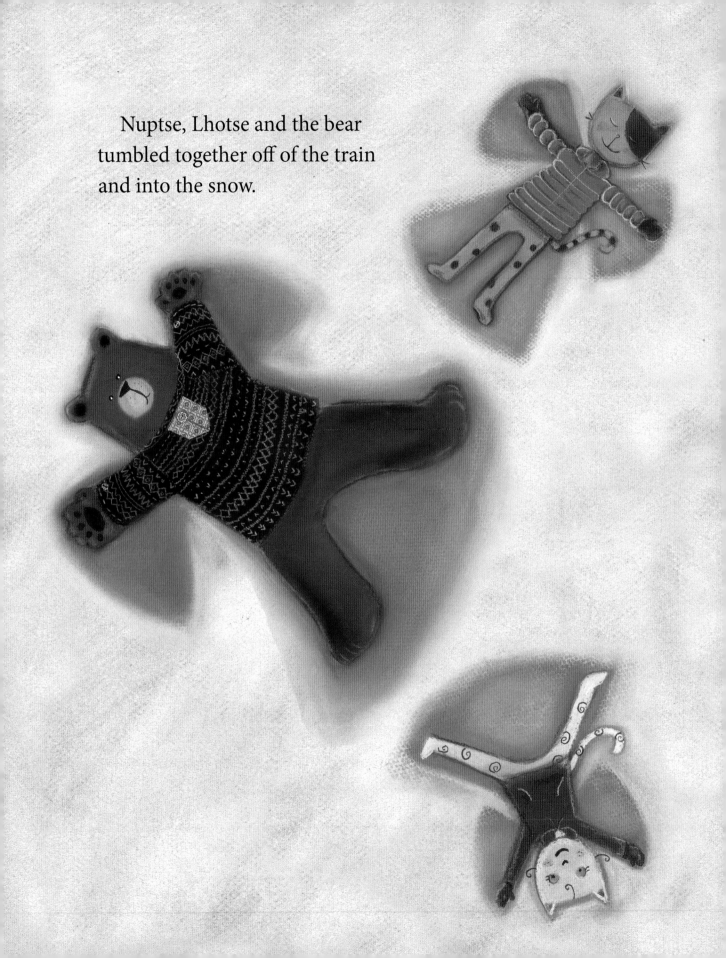

Nuptse, Lhotse and the bear
tumbled together off of the train
and into the snow.

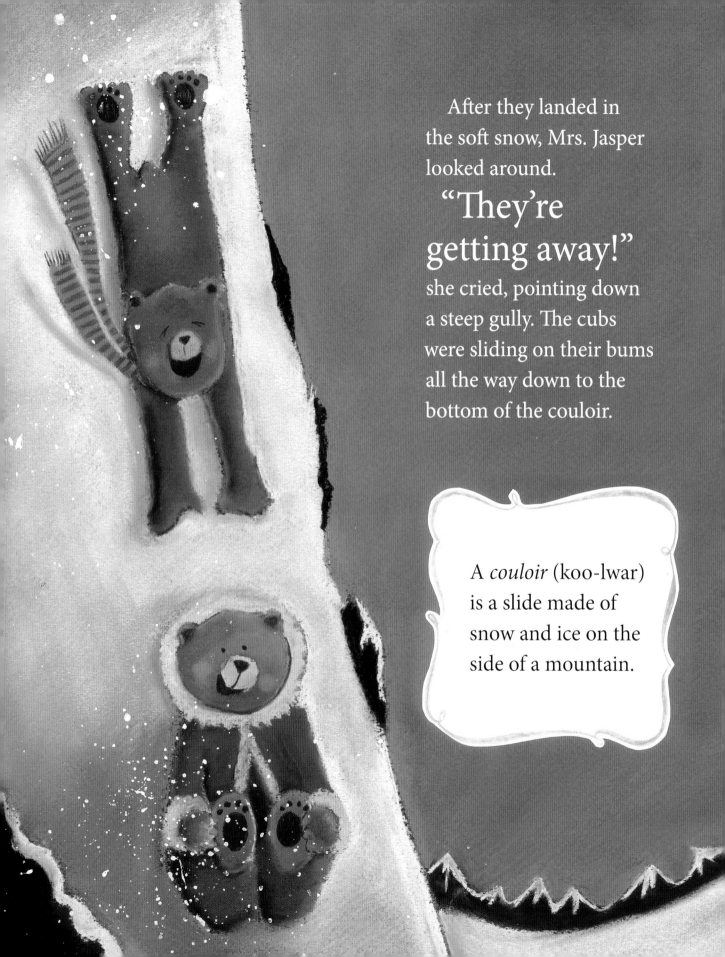

After they landed in the soft snow, Mrs. Jasper looked around. **"They're getting away!"** she cried, pointing down a steep gully. The cubs were sliding on their bums all the way down to the bottom of the couloir.

A *couloir* (koo-lwar) is a slide made of snow and ice on the side of a mountain.

"Hurry, we have
to catch them," said Lhotse.
"I have just what we need." Lhotse
opened his backpack and pulled out
skis and a snowboard. He always seemed
to have everything the cats needed.

Nuptse and Lhotse snapped on their skis
and snowboard and carved down the slope.
Mrs. Jasper rolled down after them.

Whoosh

LEGEND

● Easy Peasy
❄ Tricky Bits
◆ Crazy Hard
◆◆ Steep & Deep
▨ Out of Bounds

They tore through the trees.

They jumped over bumps

and slid to a breathless stop at the bottom.

"Do you see where Kootenay and Yoho went?"
asked Lhotse.

"There they are!" said Nuptse.
"They are chasing a giant mouse in a fur coat!"

"That's not a mouse," laughed the bear. "It's a marmot.
They live higher than most animals in the Rockies."

ANIMALS THAT SHOULD LIVE IN THE ROCKIES:

Marmots

Wolves

Owls

Porcupines

Moose

Bighorn Sheep

Mountain Goats

Caribou

Cougars

Foxes

Bears

ANIMALS THAT SHOULD LIVE FAR AWAY FROM THE ROCKIES:

Penguins
(Antarctica)

Yaks
(Asia)

Koalas (Australia)

Giraffes
(Africa)

Llamas
(South America)

Ibex
(Europe)

The cats and the bear watched the
cubs run across the sparkling snow.

"Oh, no," said Mrs. Jasper. "My little cubs have just chased that marmot right out onto the Columbia Icefield – it's the biggest glacier in the Rockies. There are hundreds of deep cracks called crevasses (kruh-yasses) hiding under the snow. How will we follow them and not fall in?"

Lhotse pointed at a machine parked beside the icefield.

"Can we use that snow car to follow them?" he asked.

"That's just what we need! **It's a Snowcat!**" exclaimed Mrs. Jasper.

They scrambled up into the Snowcat. Mrs. Jasper turned the key, and the machine glided across the ice.

START

They chased
the cubs
through the
maze of ice.

Mrs. Jasper leaned out of the
Snowcat. "Yoho and Kootenay,
I found you!" she shouted.
    The cubs turned around,
waved and disappeared.

"I think they just fell into
a crevasse," said Lhotse.

FINISH

Nuptse, Lhotse and Mrs. Jasper carefully crawled to the edge of the crevasse and looked down. The cubs smiled up at them from the bottom.

"We fell in a hole, Mommy!" they giggled.

"I wish I had brought a rope," said Lhotse.

Nuptse squealed and began opening her backpack.
"How about … this?" she asked as she pulled out the
biggest ball of string in the world.

"I can't believe you brought your string collection,"
laughed Lhotse. "Let's lower the end into the crevasse.

Everyone, *hold on tight*."

The little cubs hugged the string as Mrs. Jasper and the cats pulled them out of the crevasse.

"Mommy, we had the

biggest adventure ever!"

said Yoho.

"Who are they?" asked Kootenay, pointing at the cats.

"This is Nuptse and Lhotse. They helped me find you," said Mrs. Jasper. The cubs looked at the cats shyly and then pounced on them playfully.

"Thank you, Nuptse! Thank you, Lhotse!"

they giggled.

The mountains wore cloud coats and mist scarves that night as the bears and cats sat around a crackling campfire roasting marshmallows.

Nuptse and Lhotse sipped from their mugs of hot chocolate and whispered goodnight to Yoho and Kootenay as the cubs fell asleep in Mrs. Jasper's big bear hug.

THE END

THE BEAR FACTS

This mostly made-up story was inspired by a series of events that actually happened in the Canadian Rockies. In 2007 a trio of black bear cubs made the news when they jumped on a train to eat grain and accidentally rode from Yoho Park to Field, British Columbia (about 30 km). Park Wardens reunited the cubs with their mother, but a week later the cubs repeated this train ride. Thankfully, no bears were lost or hurt during this particular big adventure. There are many people in the Canadian Rockies who love bears very much, and you can learn more about this at www.wildsmart.ca and www.y2y.net.

ACKNOWLEDGEMENTS

I am fortunate to live in a community that has as many authors as mountains, and many of these writers have encouraged, supported and mentored me along the way. A special thank you to Jerry Auld, Jeremy Kroeker, Stephen Legault, Lori Nunn, Michael Wuitchik, Bob Sandford, Lynn Martel, Frances Klatzel, Helen Rose, Christine Thorpe and Carol McTavish for sharing your wisdom and for your friendships.

This sequel could not have been possible without all of my *Nuptse and Lhotse in Nepal* fans around the world, and especially Joy and Nina at Café Books. Thanks to Anne and Ray for your patience, care and technical support. A giant thank you to the amazing team of Don, Chyla, Cory and Heather at Rocky Mountain Books, who recognized that these cats wanted more adventures and helped make it happen!

My life is blessed with a circle of friends who have always believed in my dream to make stories. Thank you especially to my family: Eugene, Lin, Josh and Hayley, and my partner in life, travel and all things creative, Jamey Glasnovic.